The Silent Witness

For my wonderful father-in-law, Leo Friedman, Civil War buff
and accountant extraordinaire.

A thousand thanks to Patrick Schroeder, historian at Appomattox Court House National Historic Park
— R.F.

For Boto,
Our separate memories make up one past.
—C.A.N.

Text copyright © 2005 by Robin Friedman
Illustrations copyright © 2005 by Claire A. Nivola

www.houghtonmifflinbooks.com

The text of this book is set in Galliard.
The illustrations are watercolor and gauche.

Library of Congress Cataloging-in-Publication Data

Friedman, Robin, 1968–
The Silent Witness / by Robin Friedman; illustrated by Claire A. Nivola
p. cm.
10-ISBN: 0-618-44230-8
13-ISBN: 978-0-618-44230-0
1. McLean family—Juvenile literature. 2. McLean, Wilmer, 1814–1882—Juvenile literature.
3. Appomattox (Va.)—Biography—Juvenile literature. 4. Manassas (Va.)—Biography—Juvenile literature.
5. Virginia—History—Civil War, 1861–1865—Biography—Juvenile literature.
6. United States—History—Civil War, 1861–1865—Biography—Juvenile literature.
7. United States—History—Civil War, 1861–1865—Juvenile literature. I. Title.
F234.A6F75 2004
973.7'092—dc22

2004001013

Printed in Singapore
TWP 10 9 8 7 6 5 4 3 2 1

The Silent Witness

A TRUE STORY OF THE CIVIL WAR

By Robin Friedman

Illustrated by Claire A. Nivola

Houghton Mifflin Company
Boston 2005

Lula McLean lived in Manassas, Virginia, on a plantation overlooking Bull Run Creek in a peaceful countryside dotted with cedars and pines.

She lived with her mother, father, sisters, brother, and a rag doll Mama made for her.

They grew wheat, corn, and oats.

Lula loved making candy out of sorghum molasses, learning her lessons in the peach orchard, and playing with her rag doll.

When Lula was four years old, her life changed forever.

On April 12, 1861, soldiers under the command of General Pierre G. T. Beauregard fired on Fort Sumter in Charleston, South Carolina. Major Robert Anderson, who now commanded Fort Sumter, was General Beauregard's former teacher from West Point.

After thirty-four hours of nonstop bombardment, Major Anderson surrendered. The Civil War had begun.

The Civil War was fought between twenty-three states in the North, known as the Union, and thirteen states in the South, known as the Confederacy.

One of the main disagreements the Union and Confederacy had was over slavery. The North wanted to abolish it. The South wanted to preserve its way of life. When the South decided to leave the United States and form a new nation, war began.

In July 1861, General Beauregard and his forces arrived in Manassas, Virginia, where Lula and her family lived. General Beauregard wanted the McLean home as his headquarters.

Lula's father, Wilmer McLean, agreed to help the general.

When Lula looked out on her front lawn, she saw miles of men dressed in gray under the maple and hickory trees.

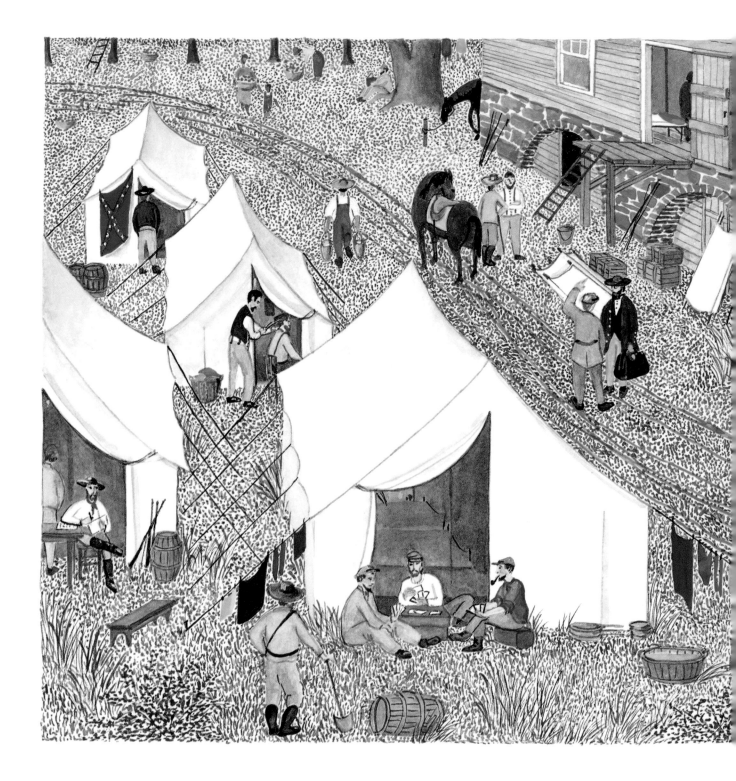

The peaceful fields where cattle once grazed became littered with trenches, tents, and cannon. The stone barn was turned into a hospital.

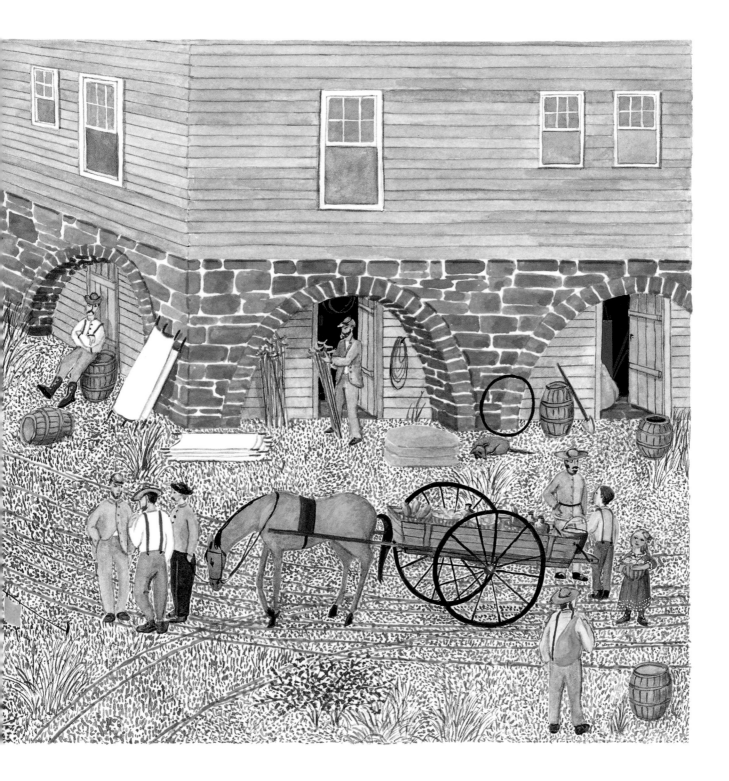

Lula and her seven-year-old brother, Wilmer Jr., helped feed the camps of the First, Eleventh, and Seventeenth regiments with a wagon loaded with pails of fresh buttermilk, baskets of bread, dozens of eggs, and a smoked hog.

On July 21, 1861, a Union cannonball tore through the McLean kitchen. It exploded in a pot of stew that was supposed to be General Beauregard's lunch. Nobody was hurt.

That summer, Union and Confederate forces fought the first major battle of the Civil War, which became known as the Battle of Bull Run in the North and Manassas in the South.

Lula's father worried about his family. With the armies fighting practically on his front lawn, he decided to move far away from the battle.

The McLeans left Manassas and moved to a smaller house in a tiny village called Appomattox Court House, 143 miles to the south.

Lula missed the plantation on the knoll amid the pasture lands.

Union forces blockaded the South's ports to prevent staples like salt, soap, and medicine from getting through. During the war, Lula and her family used raspberry leaves to make tea and burnt corn to make coffee.

Mama gave birth to Nannie. Lula let her new baby sister play with her rag doll.

For three bloody days in July 1863, more than fifty-one thousand men were killed, wounded, or captured at the Battle of Gettysburg in Pennsylvania. It was the last time the Confederacy would try to invade the North. The governor of Pennsylvania decided to create a national cemetery for the dead. A famous speaker named Edward Everett was invited. President Lincoln was invited, too.

Everett spoke for two hours. President Lincoln spoke for two minutes.

Everett's speech has long been forgotten. But the president's short speech became known as the Gettysburg Address.

In his speech, President Lincoln said, "We here highly resolve these dead shall not have died in vain, that the nation shall have a new birth of freedom, and that government of the people, by the people, for the people, shall not perish from the earth."

In May 1864, the Union general William Tecumseh Sherman marched his sixty thousand troops through the South. His soldiers set fire to farmhouses, barns, and fields. On September 2, 1864, Sherman captured Atlanta.

In the town of Appomattox Court House, families feared a Yankee invasion. They buried their silver, gold coins, and kegs of brandy to hide them from Union troops.

In December 1864, Lula helped decorate the house with greenery, holly berries, ribbons, lace, and popcorn. Wilmer Jr. placed Lula's doll on top of the Christmas tree.

General Sherman marched into Savannah and offered the city to President Lincoln as a Christmas present.

The Confederacy was losing the war.

The Confederate general Robert E. Lee and his troops were trapped outside the town of Appomattox Court House. With his army beaten and hungry, Lee decided to surrender to the Union general Ulysses S. Grant.

Lee sent Colonel Charles Marshall to look for a suitable place to meet Grant. The first man Marshall found was Wilmer McLean.

Marshall asked McLean if the generals could meet in his house.

On April 9, 1865, Lula was playing with her rag doll in the parlor.

General Lee, towering at nearly six feet tall, arrived in a spotless uniform, sash, sword, and shined boots.

General Grant arrived half an hour later wearing a slouch hat, common soldier's coat, and muddy boots.

Lula fled the room, leaving her rag doll on the horsehair sofa.

Lee surrendered to Grant in the McLean parlor.
Soldiers dubbed Lula's doll "the silent witness."

After the surrender was signed, they played catch with her, and the Union lieutenant colonel Thomas W. C. Moore stuffed her into his pocket as a souvenir.

The Civil War was over. Lula never saw her doll again.

Author's Note

Wilmer McLean could rightfully say, "The war started in my front yard and ended in my front parlor."

The story of the McLean family is true. The McLeans really did live in Manassas when the Civil War broke out. A Union cannonball really did explode in a pot of stew, and the family did move to Appomattox Court House. And, unfortunately, the war found them in their new home when Lee surrendered to Grant in their parlor.

Lula McLean, whose real name was Lucretia, had six siblings: Maria, Osceola ("Ocie"), Sarah, Wilmer Jr., Nannie, and Virginia ("Jennie"). She loved her rag doll, which was made by her mother out of coarse unbleached cotton with two inked eyes.

Lula left her beloved rag doll in her parlor on April 9, 1865, and never saw her again. Union officers made off with many of the items in the McLean parlor as souvenirs. The table where Grant and Lee wrote the terms of surrender was bought by General Philip Sheridan for twenty dollars in gold and later given to General George Armstrong Custer. Colonel Moore carried Lula's doll to New York and kept her in a glass box on his mantel as a "war trophy" for many years. In 1992, after more than 120 years, Lula's doll was donated to Appomattox Court House National Historic Park, where she is currently on permanent display.

The Civil War was the bloodiest conflict in American history. Between the war's beginning in 1861 and its end in 1865, more than six hundred thousand Americans died. More Americans died from disease and infection than from battlefield wounds.

The Civil War ushered in many firsts. During the Civil War, Americans celebrated the first official Thanksgiving in 1864, paid the first-ever federal income tax, and were drafted into the military for the first time.

President Lincoln's own son, Captain Robert Lincoln, was present at the surrender at Appomattox Court House.